I'M HAVING A Sky Blue Day!

A COLORFUL BOOK ABOUT FEELINGS

By Maggie Testa

Illustrated by Clair Rossiter

Simon Spotlight

New York   London   Toronto   Sydney   New Delhi

SIMON SPOTLIGHT

An imprint of Simon & Schuster Children's Publishing Division
1230 Avenue of the Americas, New York, New York 10020
This Simon Spotlight paperback edition February 2018
© 2018 Crayola, Easton, PA 18044-0431. Crayola®, Crayola Oval Logo®, Serpentine Design®, Vivid Violet®, Outer Space®, Laser Lemon®, Screamin'
Green®, Mauvelous®, Jazzberry Jam®, Tumbleweed®, Sunset Orange®, and Sonic Silver® are registered trademarks of Crayola used under license.
All rights reserved, including the right of reproduction in whole or in part in any form.
SIMON SPOTLIGHT and colophon are registered trademarks of Simon & Schuster, Inc.
For information about special discounts for bulk purchases, please contact Simon & Schuster Special Sales at 1-866-506-1949
or business@simonandschuster.com.
Manufactured in the United States of America 0219 LAK
10 9 8 7 6 5 4
ISBN 978-1-5344-1529-4 (hc)
ISBN 978-1-5344-1528-7 (pbk)
ISBN 978-1-5344-1530-0 (eBook)

Life is an adventure.

Each day is different from one to the next,

and there's always a surprise
waiting just around the corner.

Some days are picture perfect, and some are . . . well, *not* so perfect. But no
matter what, life is colorful. Just turn the page to explore the many shades of life!

A WONDERFUL morning !

On a wonderful morning I look up in awe—
at the beauty in a passing cloud
and the magic of a blade of grass.

I'm having a Sky Blue day!
What color feels wonderful to you?

A BRIGHT and SMILEY morning!

On a bright and smiley morning
I feel like everything is going right.

The sun is shining, the birds are singing,
and everyone is smiling—especially me!

I'm having a Vivid Violet day!
What color feels bright and smiley to you?

An ADVENTUROUS day!

On an adventurous day I dream big.
I want to scale the highest mountain,

swim in the deepest ocean,

and blast off into the great unknown.

I'm having an Outer Space day!
What color feels adventurous to you?

A LEMONADE day!

On a lemonade day life gives me sour lemons,

but I turn them into sweet lemonade!

When I take a not-so-sunny day
and try to see the good in it,

I'm having a Laser Lemon day!
What color feels like lemonade to you?

A ROLLER COASTER day!

On a roller coaster day anything can happen.

It is up
and down
and everything in between.

Buckle up for one wild ride!
I'm having a Screamin' Green day!
What color feels like a roller coaster to you?

A LOVELY day!

On a lovely day I am surrounded by those I love and those who love me.

There is a happy feeling in my heart.
I'm having a Mauvelous day!
What color feels lovely to you?

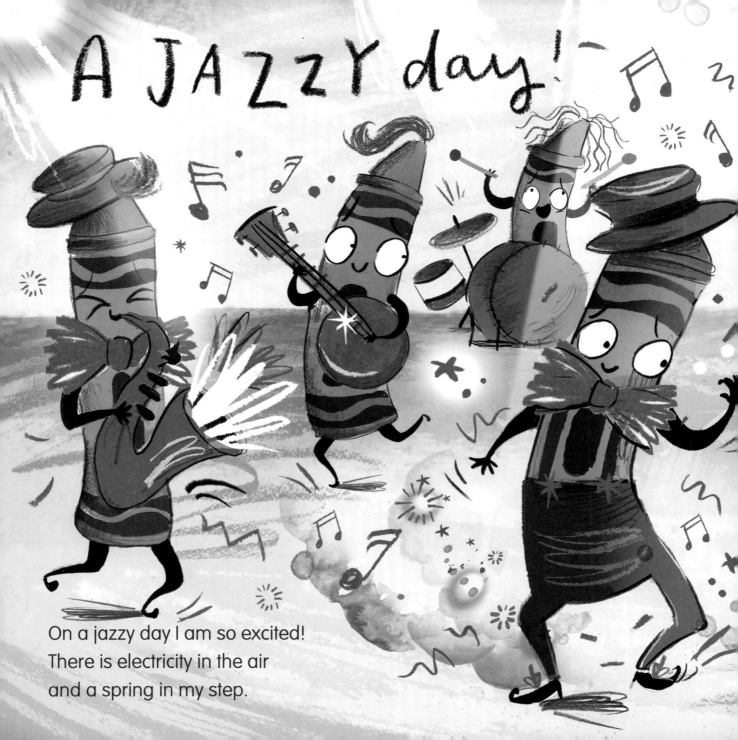

A JAZZY day!

On a jazzy day I am so excited!
There is electricity in the air
and a spring in my step.

I can't wait to see what's next.
I'm having a Jazzberry Jam day!
What color feels jazzy to you?

A RELAXING day!

On a relaxing day I enjoy the quiet.

It's a perfect day for naps,

and walking the dog,

and seeing where my imagination takes me.
I'm having a Tumbleweed day!
What color feels relaxing to you?

A PEACEFUL night!

On a peaceful night, the day is winding down.
The sun is setting in the sky, birds are in their nests,
and a feeling of peace blankets the world.

I'm having a Sunset Orange day!
What color feels peaceful to you?

A TWINKLY night!

On a twinkly night the sky is dark.

It is time to climb into bed.
The stars sparkle and shine above,
and my eyes feel heavy with sleep.

I'm having a Sonic Silver day!
What color feels twinkly to you?
I wonder what colors tomorrow will bring!

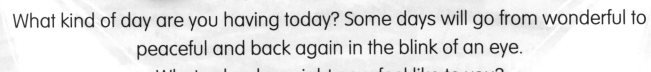

What kind of day are you having today? Some days will go from wonderful to peaceful and back again in the blink of an eye.
What color does right now feel like to you?

These days were brought to you by the crayon colors listed below. Draw pictures of your days with these colors or any ones you'd like. Use your imagination!

Sky Blue   Vivid Violet   Outer Space   Laser Lemon

Screamin' Green   Mauvelous   Jazzberry Jam   Tumbleweed

Sunset Orange   Sonic Silver